A ROOKIE READER®

SPIDERS
AND WEBS

By Carolyn Lunn

Illustrations by Tom Dunnington

Prepared under the direction of Robert Hillerich, Ph.D.

 CHILDRENS PRESS®
CHICAGO

LIBRARY OF CONGRESS
Library of Congress Cataloging-in-Publication Data

Lunn, Carolyn.
  Spiders and webs / by Carolyn Lunn ; illustrated by
Tom Dunnington.
    p.   cm. — (A Rookie reader)
  Summary: Describes, in verse, things that go
together, such as cars and trucks, swans and ducks,
balls and bats, and heads and hats.
  ISBN 0-516-02093-5
  [1. Vocabulary. 2. Stories in rhyme.] I. Dunnington,
Tom, ill. II. Title. III. Series.
PZ8.3.L9726Sp   1989
428.1—dc20   89-34665
                                                 CIP
                                                 AC

Spiders and webs go together

like clouds and sky,
cream and pie,

bread and jam,

bells and lambs,

spouts and whales, and

wags and tails!

Boys and girls go together
like cars and trucks,

swans and ducks,

umbrellas and rain,
a man with a cane,

a fork and spoon, and
stars and the moon!

Sand and shells go together
like dogs and bones,

16

ice cream and cones,

balls and bats,

20

heads and hats,

lightning and thunder, and

why and wonder!

Farmers and tractors go together

like baths and bubbles,

boots and puddles,
paint and brush,

hurry and rush,

sharing and friends, and

beginnings and ends!

WORD LIST

a	cones	lightning	stars
and	cream	like	swans
balls	dogs	man	tails
baths	ducks	moon	the
bats	ends	paint	thunder
beginnings	farmers	pie	together
bells	fork	puddles	tractors
bones	friends	rain	trucks
boots	girls	rush	umbrellas
boys	go	sand	wags
bread	hats	sharing	webs
brush	heads	shells	whales
bubbles	hurry	sky	why
cane	ice cream	spiders	with
cars	jam	spoon	wonder
clouds	lambs	spouts	

About the Author

Carolyn Lunn is an American, now living in England with her British husband and three-year-old son. As well as writing stories, she enjoys running, cooking, and gardening. Her other books include *A Whisper Is Quiet*, *Bobby's Zoo*, and *Purple Is Part of a Rainbow*.

About the Artist

Tom Dunnington divides his time between book illustration and wildlife painting. He has done many books for Childrens Press, as well as working on textbooks, and is a regular contributor to "Highlights for Children." Tom lives in Oak Park, Illinois.